SOMEWHERE A BELL IS RINGING

story & pictures by Barbara Nye

penny candy BOOKS

Penny Candy Books
Oklahoma City & Savannah
© 2017 Barbara Nye

SUSTAINABLE
FORESTRY
INITIATIVE
Certified Chain of Custody
Promoting Sustainable Forestry
www.sfiprogram.org
SFI-01268
SFI label applies to the text stock

The Sustainable Forestry Initiative® program integrates the perpetual growing and harvesting of trees with the protection of wildlife, plants, soils and water.

Design: Shanna Compton, shannacompton.com

Photo of Barbara Nye by Christopher Irons

21 20 19 18 17   1 2 3 4 5
ISBN-13: 978-0-9972219-6-1 (paperback)
ISBN-13: 978-0-9987999-2-6 (hardcover)

Books for the kid in *all* of us
www.pennycandybooks.com

This book is dedicated to Naomi Shihab Nye, whose ways and words
are an endless inspiration; and to Christopher, Grace, Hillary,
and Woodley, who light up the path.

Somewhere a bell is ringing
in a busy marketplace

where a lady in a yellow dress
buys lettuces and lace.

Somewhere the rain is falling
with a happy tapping sound

on a rock above a speckled frog
who's burrowed in the ground.

Somewhere an old truck rattles down a bumpy country track

and children run to see the big green melons in the back.

Somewhere a boat is sailing over green and glassy waves.

Far below a spotted eel emerges from his caves.

Somewhere a river rushes past
a painted yellow bridge

Somewhere thunder cracks and rolls across a darkened plain,

and safe inside her tiny hut
the farmer hopes for rain.

Somewhere the sun is blazing down
on shining desert land,

and a lizard scampers lightly
over burning golden sand.

Somewhere a gate is creaking, and a visitor comes through

with flowers from her garden,
the way that friends will do.

Somewhere a drum is beating on a crowded city street.

Two bankers on their way to work
have stopped to tap their feet.

Somewhere the aurora weaves its colors through the sky

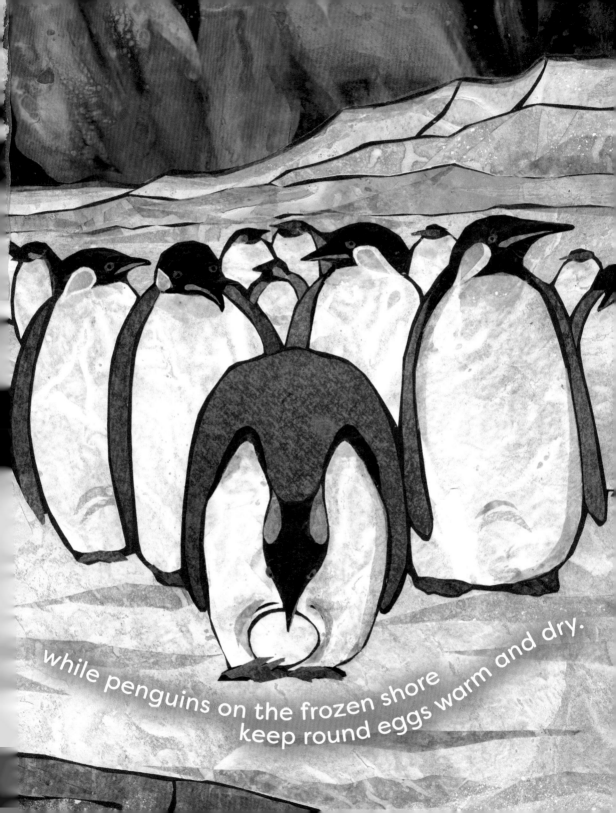

while penguins on the frozen shore
keep round eggs warm and dry.

Somewhere the news is buzzing
in a café on the square,

and the smell of spicy tea
is rising up to fill the air.

Somewhere a boulder crashes down a rocky mountainside.

A little mouse pricks up his ears and scurries off to hide.

Somewhere music's playing on a radio upstairs,

and a man who wears a checkered vest
is slicing up some pears.

Somewhere the grass is waving
in the early morning breeze.

On his way, a yellow dog has stopped to scratch his fleas.

Somewhere a road is humming
        as the cars rush by so fast

and a group of friends will share their soup
and tell of thoughts and dreams.

Somewhere against a canyon wall water splashes down,

and a turtle climbs up on a log
and gazes all around.

Somewhere a clock is ticking
in a cabin near a lake,

and a cat beside the fireplace
just can't quite stay awake.

Somewhere far across the world
in brilliant morning sun

a bell is ringing in the square;
the day has just begun.

But here the stars are twinkling,
and the moon is shining bright.

It's time for sleep, it's time to dream,
and it's time to say . . .

. . . good night.

Originally from Cyclone, Texas, **Barbara Nye** has been strongly influenced in her artwork by her travels in many countries and her experiences living in South America and Canada. She has a degree in Spanish and Latin American studies from the University of Texas at Austin and is fluent in Spanish. Barbara has lived in Australia for over 25 years, has been an Australian citizen since 1992, and raised her three children there.

As a self-taught artist, Barbara combines her skills as a colorist, painter, and innovator. Also a textile artist, she uses machine embroidery over hand-painted papers in many of her works. Barbara believes art should have an element of fun, both for the creator and for the viewer.

Barbara works from original drawings, creating her colorful pictures by cutting thousands of pieces of hand-painted paper of various weights and types. The papers all start out white, and she dips, stamps, prints, and glazes with acrylic paints to achieve interesting patterns. She then cuts the papers to the shapes in her original drawings. Barbara worked this process out over many years of experimentation. People say, "It must take patience," but for Barbara it is fun from start to finish!